For Keith – MR

For Sonny – MB

Published in the UK by Scholastic, 2022
1 London Bridge, London, SE1 9BG
Scholastic Ireland, 89E Lagan Road, Dublin Industrial Estate,
Glasnevin, Dublin, D11 HP5F

SCHOLASTIC and associated logos are trademarks and/or
registered trademarks of Scholastic Inc.

Text © Michelle Robinson, 2022
Illustrations © Mike Byrne, 2022

The right of Michelle Robinson and Mike Byrne to be identified
as the author and illustrator of this work has been asserted by them
under the Copyright, Designs and Patents Act 1988.

PB ISBN 978 0702 31046 1
A CIP catalogue record for this book is available from the British Library.

Printed in Italy
Paper made from wood grown in sustainable forests and other controlled sources

3 5 7 9 10 8 6 4 2

www.scholastic.co.uk

FSC
www.fsc.org
MIX
Paper | Supporting
responsible forestry
FSC® C023419

THE PUMPKIN WHO WAS AFRAID OF THE DARK

Michelle
Robinson

Mike
Byrne

SCHOLASTIC

The way **every** pumpkin is **meant** to behave
is **fearless** and **feisty** and **spooky** and **brave**.
It's what every pumpkin is happy to do . . .

apart from the littlest pumpkin
named Boo.

Boo isn't **spooky**.
She's small and she's **sweet**.

"I don't want to dress up
and play trick or treat!

I'm afraid of the dark!
I don't like Halloween!"

She's the **least** scary pumpkin
the world's **ever** seen.

Her friends are excited.

"Tonight's the **big** night!
We get to pull faces
and give folks a **fright**!
What are YOU going as, Boo?
Do you know?"

"I'm frightened of ghosts
and I'm frightened of bats.
I'm frightened of witches
in big pointy hats.

And trying to scare people
just sounds so mean.
I'm afraid of the dark!
I don't like Halloween!"

The others get picked.
Boo is all on her **own**.
"I'm starting to wish that
I'd never been sown."

From out of the **gloom** comes a **terrible**

SCREEEEAM

"It's so **creepy** and **dark.** I don't like Halloween!"

Boo **shakes** from the tip of her stalk to her roots
as up to the patch **stomps** a **witch** in black boots,

with a mop for a **broom** and a **big** cardboard hat,
and a **cute** little brother who's dressed as a **bat**.

"Pick out a pumpkin,"
the witch says,
        "let's go!"

But her brother
the bat
shakes his head
and says . . .

"NO!"

"I'm **frightened** of monsters
with **big** pointy teeth!
I'm **frightened** of graveyards
with **bones** underneath!

That **pumpkin's** the **spookiest**
I've **ever** seen!
I'm afraid of the dark!
I don't like Halloween!"

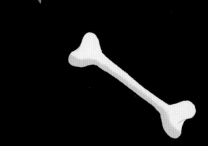

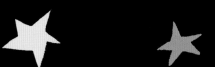

Boo can't believe it. Could it really be . . . ?

"You certainly needn't feel frightened of me.

I'm small and I'm **sweet**!
Let me lend you my light
to help you feel safe
on this dark, **spooky** night."

Boo starts to **glow**. She feels **BIG!** She feels **BRAVE!**
She behaves as a pumpkin is **meant** to behave.

Fearless and **feisty**

and – most of all – **FUN**.

Her **Halloween** party
has **finally** begun!

The little bat says,
"I'm **not** scared thanks to you.
What's your name, pumpkin . . . ?"

Boo grins
and shouts . . .

"BOO!"